MODERN CURRICULUM PRESS
CLEVELAND • TORONTO

MCP **MODERN CURRICULUM PRESS**
Cleveland • Toronto

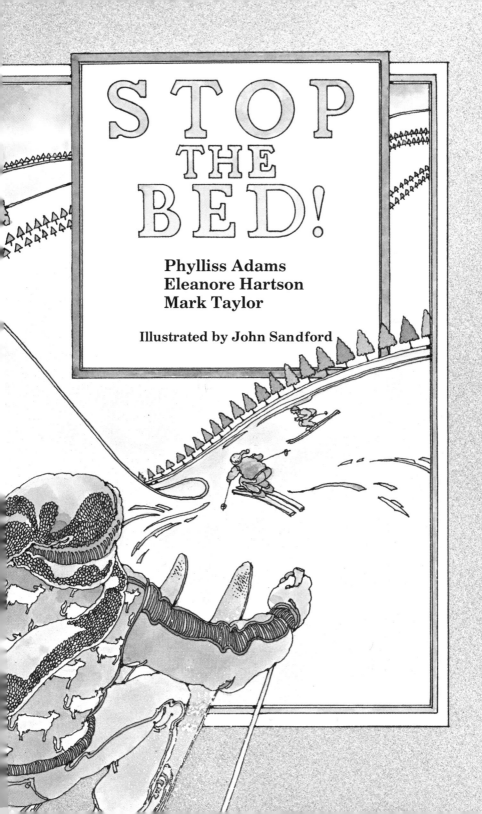

STOP THE BED!

Phylliss Adams
Eleanore Hartson
Mark Taylor

Illustrated by John Sandford

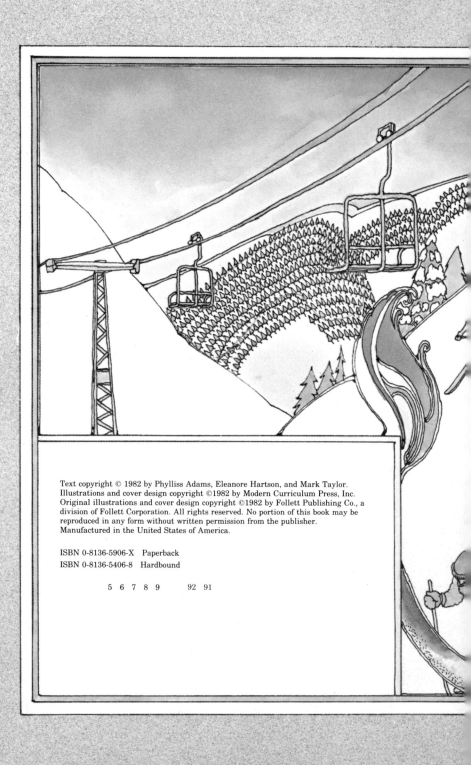

ISBN 0-8136-5906-X Paperback
ISBN 0-8136-5406-8 Hardbound

      5   6   7   8   9   92 91

"I love to ski," said Cora Cow.

"Here we go," said Cora.
"Up and up and up.
We ride up.
We will ski down."

"I will ski down here," Cora said.

"Can we all ski down here, Dad?"
said Danny.

"Yes," said Dad.
"And here I go."

"And here I go," said Danny.

"And here I go," said Cora.

"Down and down we all go,"
said Cora.
"Down and down."

"Look out," said Dad.
"Look out, Danny!"

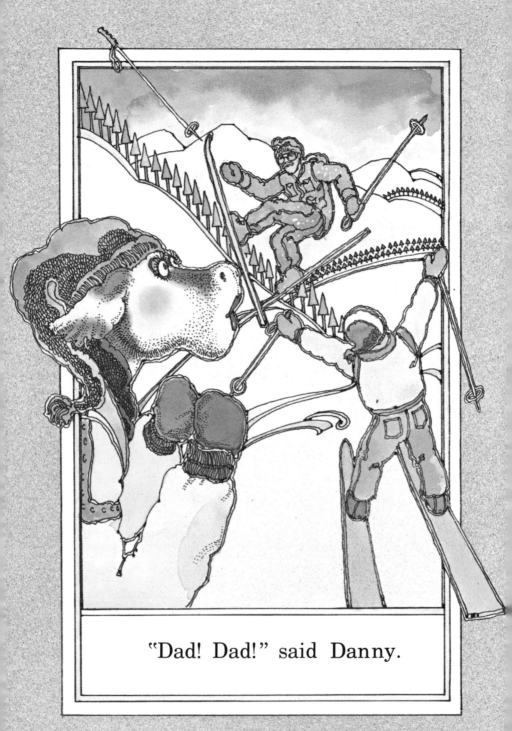

"Dad! Dad!" said Danny.

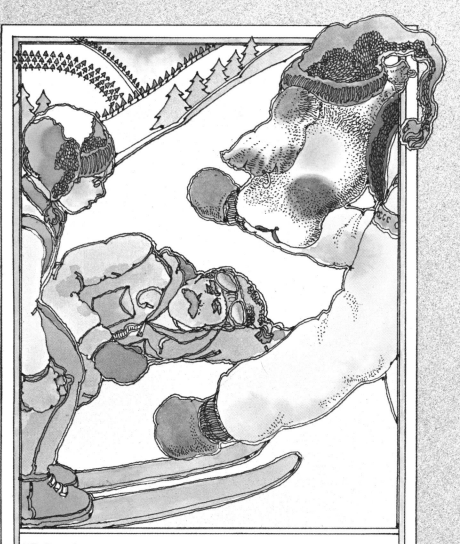

"My leg. My leg," said Dad.

"What will we do, Cora?" said Danny.

"We will do what we can," said Cora.

"Look, Danny," said Cora.
"See that little house?
I will go there for help."

"No one is here," said Cora.
"But I see something that will help."

"Come here, Danny," Cora said.
"Please come and help with this bed.
A bed will work."

"Cora," said Dad.
"You are some cow!"

"Cora to the rescue!" said Danny.

"A bed to the rescue!" said Cora.

"Cora, can you stop the bed?"
said Danny.

"I can not stop it," said Cora.
"But I will find a way."

"Here we are," said Cora.

"What a ride!" said Danny.

"And what a rescue!"
said Dad.

"I love to go to the rescue,"
said Cora.
"And I do!"

Ride Up and Ski Down!

If necessary, read these directions to the child:
Start at Up. Read each sign on the ride up.
Then find the way down. Read each sign on
the way down.

Stop here.

Look down.
What do you see?

This way up.

Up

You will love
to ski down.

Look out!

Yes, you are down.

27

What Will Work?

Cora and Danny want to get the truck out.
What will help them?

Cora and Danny want to ride down.
What can they ride on?

Danny and Dad

Look at each picture.
Tell what you think Danny and Dad are saying.

All the words that appear in the story *Stop the Bed!* are listed here.

a	find	no	up
all	for	not	
and			way
are	go	one	we
	help	out	what
bed	here		will
but	house	please	with
			work
can	I	rescue	
come	is	ride	yes
Cora Cow	it		you
cow		said	
	leg	see	
Dad	little	ski	
Danny	look	some	
do	love	something	
down		stop	
	my		
		that	
		the	
		there	
		this	
		to	

About the Authors

Phylliss Adams, Eleanore Hartson, and Mark Taylor have a combined background that includes writing books for children and teachers, teaching at the elementary and university levels, and working in the areas of curriculum development, reading instruction and research, teacher training, parent education, and library and media services.

About the Illustrator

Since attending the American Academy of Art in Chicago, Illinois, John Sandford has concentrated on illustration for books and magazines.

The artist works in Chicago, where he lives with his wife, Frances. The illustrations for Cora Cow were executed in the spirit of the artist's father, who left to the Sandford family the rich legacy of his creativity.